T

NOV 30 2016

W9-CRZ-064

12 REASONS TO LOVE THE
CHICAGO CUBS

by Todd Kortemeier

www.12StoryLibrary.com

12-Story Library is an imprint of Peterson Publishing Company and Press Room Editions.

Produced for 12-Story Library by Red Line Editorial

Photographs ©: Warren Wimmer/Icon Sportswire/AP Images, cover, 1, 13, 29; Dmitrijs Bindemanis/Shutterstock Images, 4; Amy Sancetta/AP Images, 5; AP Images, 6, 7, 18; Eric Risberg/AP Images, 9; Beth A. Keiser/AP Images, 11; Fred Jewell/AP Images, 15, 28; Pete Leabo/AP Images, 16; Nam Y. Huh/AP Images, 17; Charles Bennett/AP Images, 19; George Grantham Bain Collection/Library of Congress, 20; HO/AP Images, 21; Scott Boehm/AP Images, 23; Paul Beaty/AP Images, 24; iofoto/Shutterstock Images, 25; Jeff Roberson/AP Images, 27

ISBN
978-1-63235-210-1 (hardcover)
978-1-63235-237-8 (paperback)
978-1-62143-262-3 (hosted ebook)

Library of Congress Control Number: 2015934315

Printed in the United States of America
Mankato, MN
October, 2015

Go beyond the book. Get free, up-to-date content on this topic at 12StoryLibrary.com.

TABLE OF CONTENTS

A Billy Goat Curses the Cubs 4

Mr. Cub Says, "Let's Play Two!" 6

Harry Caray Gives Fans a Voice 8

Slammin' Sammy Swings for 66 10

Wrigley Turns 100 12

Kerry Strikes Out 20 14

Cubs Become the Loveable Losers 16

Cubs Retire Six Numbers 18

Things Were Great Back in 1908 20

Cubs Wave the Flag of Victory 22

Fans Flock to Wrigleyville 24

Cubs Usher in a New Era in Wrigleyville 26

12 Key Dates 28

Glossary 30

For More Information 31

Index 32

About the Author 32

A BILLY GOAT CURSES THE CUBS

William "Billy Goat" Sianis had an idea. The Chicago Cubs were playing in the 1945 World Series. And Sianis, a local restaurant owner, had a lucky goat named Murphy. So he decided to bring the lucky pet to Game 4 at Wrigley Field.

Not everybody was thrilled. Sianis and Murphy were stopped at the gate. No goats allowed. Offended, Sianis "cursed"   the team right then. He declared the Cubs would never win a World Series unless the goat was allowed in Wrigley Field.

The Cubs had been one of baseball's better teams. Since then, however, the Cubs have won just one playoff series. They haven't been back to the World Series, either.

Anyone who questions "The Curse of the Billy Goat" need look no further

The Cubs refused to let a billy goat attend the 1945 World Series.

than the 2003 playoffs. The Cubs hosted the Florida Marlins in Game 6 of the National League Championship Series (NLCS). A win would move the Cubs to the World Series. They even had a 3–0 lead in the top of the eighth. Then things went awry.

The Marlins' Luis Castillo hit a foul ball toward the left field stands. Cubs outfielder Moises Alou went to the wall to try to catch the ball. Instead, a Cubs fan got in the way. The ball fell into the stands. Florida went on to score eight runs in the inning, win the game, and then win Game 7. It was the closest the Cubs had gotten since 1945.

2
World Series wins for the Cubs. They won in 1907 and 1908.

- The Cubs won 10 National League (NL) pennants from 1906 to 1945.
- From 1876 to 1945, the Cubs had a winning percentage of .559.
- From 1946 through 2014, the Cubs had a winning percentage of just .467.

THINK ABOUT IT

This "curse" is an example of a superstition. That is a belief in something that could be magic or not natural. Do you believe the curse is real? Even if it's not real, how might it affect the players and fans?

MR. CUB SAYS, "LET'S PLAY TWO!"

Ernie Banks spent his entire career, from 1953 to 1971, with the Cubs. Not many of those seasons were great. The Cubs had a winning record in just six of Banks's seasons. They never made the postseason.

Yet Banks always showed up, excited to play. "It's a beautiful day for a ballgame," he'd say. "Let's play two!" That dedication and enthusiasm has earned "Mr. Cub" a special place in the hearts of many fans.

Ernie Banks in 1971

Ernie Banks turns a double play against the St. Louis Cardinals.

Banks began his career in the Negro Leagues. Major League Baseball (MLB) teams refused to sign black players for many years. Jackie Robinson became the first black major leaguer in 1947. Banks became the Cubs' first black player in 1953. He proved to be one of the best.

After beginning as a shortstop, Banks later moved to first base. He was a star at both positions. Banks won two NL Most Valuable Player (MVP) Awards. He hit at least 40 home runs four seasons in a row. Plus, he was an 11-time All-Star. It was little surprise when he was elected to the Baseball Hall of Fame on his first ballot in 1977.

Yet Banks was more than a baseball star to many Cubs fans. He was a gracious ambassador for the team and the city. Long after retiring, the cheerful Banks could still be found engaging with fans around Chicago.

512
Career home runs for Ernie Banks.

- Banks's 2,528 career games is the most in Cubs history.
- Banks became the first NL player to win back-to-back MVP Awards, which he did in 1958 and 1959.
- The Cubs retired Banks's No. 14 jersey.

7

HARRY CARAY GIVES FANS A VOICE

Harry Caray had a long broadcasting career. He is most known for his time with the Cubs. He called their games on radio and TV from 1982 until his death in 1998. Some broadcasters try to stay neutral. They don't cheer for or against either team. Caray wasn't one of them.

He always rooted for the team he was covering, especially the Cubs. Whenever he worked a home game, Caray sang "Take Me Out to the Ball Game" during the seventh-inning stretch. He had many trademark sayings, as well. One of the most famous was when he'd shout, "Holy cow!" His home run call also became well known. He'd exclaim, "It might be! It could be! It *is* a home run!" Caray's unique style helped him develop a bond with Cubs fans.

Caray also developed a bond with fans outside the ballpark. He opened a famous restaurant in Chicago. If not there, he could often be found at other restaurants hanging out with Cubs fans.

The Sporting News named Caray its Baseball Announcer of the Year seven times. He also won the Ford C. Frick Award in 1989. The National Baseball Hall of Fame gives out that award to a broadcaster for "major contributions to baseball."

8,300
Approximate number of games Harry Caray broadcast in his 53-year career.

- Caray didn't miss a game in first 41 seasons.
- He worked for the St. Louis Cardinals, Oakland Athletics, and Chicago White Sox before joining the Cubs.

Harry Caray interviews Cubs second baseman Ryne Sandberg in 1996.

In 2004, the Cubs honored Caray with a statue outside Wrigley Field. The seventh-inning stretch tradition continues. Today celebrities and other sports personalities sing the song in Caray's place.

"The Cubs fans loved him, the White Sox fans loved him, the Cardinals fans loved him," legendary Cardinals player Stan Musial once said. "He was the life of the party, the life of baseball."

SLAMMIN' SAMMY SWINGS FOR 66

Sammy Sosa came to the Cubs from the crosstown Chicago White Sox in 1992. He showed promise his first year. The young outfielder hit eight home runs in just 67 games. But the next year he broke out and slugged 33 homers. Over the next few years, he developed into an MVP-level player. From 1995 to 1997 he averaged more than 37 home runs and 113 runs batted in (RBIs).

Then came 1998. Sosa and St. Louis Cardinals slugger Mark McGwire hit homer after homer. Both were on pace to break the single-season record of 61.

THINK ABOUT IT

Baseball players began hitting more home runs than ever before during the 1990s. It later came out that many of them had used PEDs to help their performance. Most now believe those players were cheating. But others note that many pitchers were also using PEDs. How do you think those players should be remembered in history? Should the home run records be counted in the record books?

42

Average number of home runs Sammy Sosa hit during his 13 seasons with the Cubs.

- His 20 homers in June 1998 set a major league record for home runs in a month.
- Sosa led the NL in homers in 2000 and 2002.
- Barry Bonds set a new single-season record with 73 homers in 2001.

People who normally didn't follow baseball tuned in. Sosa ended with 66 home runs. That was just behind McGwire's 70. But Sosa led the Cubs to the playoffs and also won the NL MVP Award.

Sosa continued slugging the ball out of the park. He surpassed 60 home runs twice more in the next three years. In all Sosa hit 609 home runs—545 with the Cubs. But not all fans remember Sosa fondly. He was later accused of cheating by using performance-enhancing drugs (PEDs).

Cubs slugger Sammy Sosa hits his 61st home run of the 1998 season.

WRIGLEY TURNS 100

Weegham Park opened on Chicago's north side on April 23, 1914. The home team, the Chicago Federals, became the Chicago Whales in 1915. Then they merged with the Cubs in 1916. Weegham Park, meanwhile, is still standing. Today it's called Wrigley Field. The Cubs have played home games there since April 20, 1916.

Wrigley Field has been the site of some of baseball's most famous moments. In 1932, the Cubs played the New York Yankees in the World Series. The Yankees' Babe Ruth stepped up to bat in Game 3. Legend has it that Ruth pointed to center field and then hit a monster home run to the exact spot. Many years later at Wrigley, the Cincinnati Reds' Pete Rose got his 4,191st career hit. That tied Ty Cobb for baseball's all-time hits record.

Wrigley Field has also seen a lot of Cubs losses. But fans always pack "The Friendly Confines." That's because the ballpark is simply a great place to watch baseball.

NOT JUST A BASEBALL PARK

Wrigley is best known for baseball. However, the ballpark has hosted many other events over the years, sports and otherwise. The Chicago Bears football team called Wrigley home until 1970. The ballpark has also hosted soccer, boxing, and hockey events over the years. Wrigley has also hosted many music concerts.

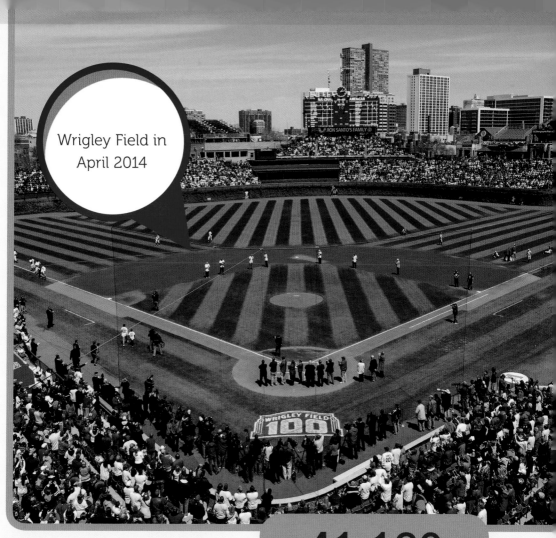

Wrigley Field in April 2014

Wrigley has several old-fashioned touches. The scoreboard is still operated by hand. Ivy grows along the outfield wall. In the spirit of baseball tradition, no night games were played at Wrigley until 1988. The stadium didn't even have lights before then.

41,160
Seating capacity of Wrigley Field.

- The Cubs led the NL in attendance nine times since moving to Wrigley Field through 2014.
- The record single-season attendance at Wrigley was 3.3 million fans in 2008.

KERRY STRIKES OUT 20

The 1998 season was a special one for Cubs fans. The team won 90 games and made the playoffs for the first time since 1989. Sammy Sosa hit 66 home runs. And on May 6, a young Cub named Kerry Wood pitched one of the most dominant games in baseball history.

In just his fifth career start, Wood beat the Houston Astros 2–0. The complete-game masterpiece took just 2 hours, 19 minutes. Wood threw 122 pitches. Most memorably, though, he struck out 20 batters. That tied a major league record.

The Astros managed just one hit. It was a single that didn't make it out of the infield. Three Astros struck out three times. Four others struck out twice. The Astros were a good team that season, too. They won

102 games and scored the most runs in the NL.

Wood was that year's NL Rookie of the Year. He finished the season with a 13–6 record and 3.40 earned-run average (ERA). Injuries limited Wood later on. But over 12 years with the Cubs, he went on to win 80 games.

5

Batters in a row that Kerry Wood struck out to start the game.

- He later struck out five in a row again.
- The Astros' Ricky Gutierrez recorded the game's only hit in the third inning.
- Wood did not walk a batter (but did hit Craig Biggio with a pitch).
- No batters reached on an error.

Kerry Wood delivers a pitch against the Houston Astros on May 6, 1998.

CUBS BECOME THE LOVEABLE LOSERS

The Cubs have had success. They won two World Series and 16 NL pennants. But all of that occurred before 1945. Their last World Series win was in 1908. Sure, they had a few good seasons after that. They won 97 games in 2008, for example. But the long wait for a championship has earned them a reputation as the "Loveable Losers."

The Cubs have experienced their share of heartbreaking defeats. One of the most notable losses was in 1984. The Cubs led the San Diego Padres two games to none in the NLCS. They needed just one more win to move on to the World Series. Chicago had a lead in each of the next three games. But the Cubs ended up dropping all three.

Cubs fans have waited a long time for a third championship. They refuse to abandon their team, though. Even in 2012, when the Cubs lost 101 games, they still attracted 2.8 million fans to Wrigley Field. Only four NL teams drew more.

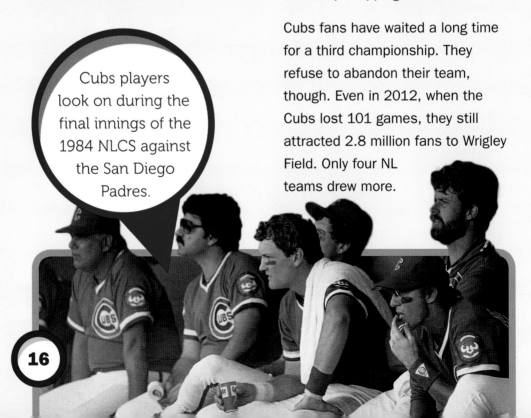

Cubs players look on during the final innings of the 1984 NLCS against the San Diego Padres.

WRIGLEY FIELD HOME OF CHICAGO CUBS

SEASON OF HOPE

Cubs fans have often had to believe in a brighter future.

8

Seasons in which the Cubs have drawn at least 3 million fans.

- The Cubs had winning records in just four of those seasons.
- The crosstown Chicago White Sox last sold more tickets than the Cubs in 1992.

FANS FROM ALL OVER

The Cubs are one of the most popular teams in baseball, successful or not. Part of this is due to the Cubs' long relationship with WGN. For many years, Cubs games were broadcast nationally on that cable channel. The Cubs also benefit from playing in Chicago. It is the third-largest city in the United States. The Cubs have many well-known celebrity fans. Among them are actor Vince Vaughn and Chicago Mayor Rahm Emanuel.

CUBS RETIRE SIX NUMBERS

Ernie Banks entertained Cubs fans for 19 seasons. So the Cubs honored the star shortstop by retiring his No. 14 jersey in 1982. That meant no future Cubs player could wear Banks's number.

The Cubs have since retired five more jerseys. Next was Billy Williams's No. 26 in 1987. That was the same year the left fielder was inducted into the Baseball Hall of Fame. Ron Santo's No. 10 was retired in 2003. He had been an All-Star third baseman for the Cubs in the 1960s and 1970s. Santo later was a Cubs broadcaster from 1990 to 2010.

The Cubs' Billy Williams raises his cap to fans in 1969.

2,038
Ferguson Jenkins's strikeouts while with the Cubs, a team record.

- All six Cubs players with retired numbers are in the Baseball Hall of Fame.
- Greg Maddux won the first of his four Cy Young Awards in 1992 while with the Cubs.

Ryne Sandberg turns a double play for the Cubs in a 1986 game.

Second baseman Ryne Sandberg was next. His No. 23 was retired in 2005. Like Williams, Sandberg was inducted into the hall of fame that same year.

The Cubs retired No. 31 in 2009. That number actually represented two great pitchers. Greg Maddux began his hall-of-fame career with the Cubs. Ferguson "Fergie" Jenkins won the 1971 NL Cy Young Award as the league's best pitcher. In addition, all major league teams retired No. 42 in 1997. Jackie Robinson, who broke baseball's color line in 1947, had worn that number.

WRIGLEY HONORS

The retired numbers have been given special places at Wrigley Field. Willie Banks's, Ron Santo's, and Ferguson Jenkins's numbers are displayed on flags flying from the left field foul pole. Billy Williams's, Ryne Sandberg's, and Greg Maddux's numbers are on flags on the right field pole. In addition, the signature home run call from former Cubs broadcaster Jack Brickhouse, "Hey Hey," is written on each foul pole.

THINGS WERE GREAT BACK IN 1908

The Cubs weren't always baseball's loveable losers. In the early 1900s, they were one of baseball's best teams. Their run from 1906 to 1908 was one of the best in baseball history.

The 1906 Cubs won 116 games. That's still a major league record, since tied by the 2001 Seattle Mariners. However, the Cubs lost to the Chicago White Sox in that year's World Series. One year

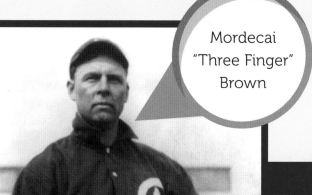

Mordecai "Three Finger" Brown

THINK ABOUT IT

The 2001 Seattle Mariners tied the 1906 Cubs' record by winning 116 games. However, the Mariners played seven more games than the Cubs. Do you think it's fair that the teams officially share the record, even though the Mariners played more games? List three reasons for why you believe so.

The 1906 Chicago Cubs

later, the Cubs won 107 games. And this time they won the World Series, too. Chicago beat the Detroit Tigers in five games. The Cubs won four and tied one.

530

Wins by the Cubs from 1906 to 1910. That was the best in MLB.

- The Cubs won four pennants and two World Series.
- The Philadelphia Athletics beat the Cubs 4–1 in 1910 World Series.
- Mordecai Brown, Frank Chance, Johnny Evers, and Joe Tinker all went to the hall of fame.

Then the Cubs became the first team to win back-to-back World Series. This time they beat Detroit 4–1. Pitcher Mordecai "Three Finger" Brown led the 1908 Cubs. He won 29 games, which is still a team record. The Cubs also had one of the best infields in baseball. First baseman Frank Chance also managed the team. He was joined by second baseman Johnny Evers and shortstop Joe Tinker. Evers hit .300 and struck out just 14 times in 1908.

The three-year run was over. But the Cubs continued to regularly contend until 1945. That's when the "curse" began.

CUBS WAVE THE FLAG OF VICTORY

Wrigley Field is baseball's second-oldest stadium. Only Boston's Fenway Park is older. Many traditions have been established in Wrigley's lifetime.

One occurs after every home game. The Cubs raise a flag above the center field scoreboard. A white flag with a blue "W" means the Cubs won. A blue flag with a white "L" means the Cubs lost.

The tradition has become one of the most popular among Cubs fans. Wrigley Field celebrated its 100th birthday in 2014. The flag ceremony was one of the candidates for "Best Tradition" during that celebration. The Cubs even sell copies of the white flag. That allows fans to celebrate a Cubs victory in the same way they do at Wrigley.

The Cubs added an additional white flag on April 24, 2008. It celebrated the team's 10,000th win.

"GO CUBS GO"

Chicago native Steve Goodman wrote the song "Go Cubs Go" in 1984. The team now plays it at Wrigley Field after a Cubs win.

2

Years between the opening of Boston's Fenway Park and Wrigley Field. Fenway opened in 1912.

- The white flag tradition began in the 1940s.
- The Cubs installed the manually operated scoreboard in 1937.
- Wrigley Field's signature ivy was also planted in 1937.

Fans hold up a white "W" flag at a 2010 Cubs game.

FANS FLOCK TO WRIGLEYVILLE

The neighborhood surrounding Wrigley Field is known as Wrigleyville. And it's a real neighborhood. Just beyond the outfield fence at Wrigley are Waveland and Sheffield Avenues. Long home runs have shattered the windows of houses across

Bleachers atop some of the buildings in Wrigleyville allow views into Wrigley Field.

15

Buildings that offer rooftop seating for Cubs home games.

- The Cubs didn't add lights to Wrigley Field until 1988 in part so they wouldn't disturb local residents.
- Many famous restaurants surround Wrigley Field.

BLEACHER SEATS

Some buildings on Waveland and Sheffield avenues have built bleacher seats on the roof. This allows fans see into Wrigley Field from across the street. The owners of these buildings charge admission, just like regular tickets. The rooftops are a long way from home plate. Yet Cubs outfielder Glenallen Hill hit a home run to a rooftop in left field in 2000.

the streets. Some nearby buildings even have bleachers on their roofs. Fans can sit there and watch Cubs games. Wrigleyville is a popular neighborhood even when the Cubs aren't playing.

Most fans come to Wrigley Field by public transportation. Chicago's famous "El" (short for elevated railway) stops just a few blocks from the ballpark. The stop provides great views of right field and the scoreboard.

Wrigley Field is a short train ride from downtown Chicago.

CUBS USHER IN A NEW ERA IN WRIGLEYVILLE

The Cubs were in a slump. They had won 97 games in 2008. Then, for the next four years, they won fewer and fewer games. The team bottomed out with 61 wins in 2012. It was time for a change.

The team hired Theo Epstein to run the organization before that 2012 season. He had turned around another "cursed" team, the Boston Red Sox. They won their first World Series in 86 years in 2004.

Epstein began putting together a talented young squad in Chicago. First baseman Anthony Rizzo and shortstop Starlin Castro made the 2014 All-Star Game. Then, before the next season, manager Joe Maddon signed with the Cubs. He had led the Tampa Bay Rays to the 2008 World Series. Many believed he was one of the best managers in baseball. The Cubs got another

NAME CHANGES

The Cubs have been around since 1876. They've only been called the Cubs since 1903, though. The team began as the White Stockings (no relation to today's Chicago White Sox). It took the name Colts in 1890. Then, from 1898 to 1902, the team was called the Chicago Orphans. The team changed its name to Cubs because it had many young players at the time.

1,282

Games won by former Cubs manager Cap Anson, a team record.

- Anson managed the Cubs from 1879 to 1897.
- Anson was also a hall of fame player for the Cubs from 1876 to 1897.

big boost in 2015. Talented young third baseman Kris Bryant joined the team. For Cubs fans, these were signs that the curse might soon be over.

Cubs rookie Kris Bryant rounds third base to score in a 2015 game.

12 KEY DATES

1876

The Cubs are founded as the Chicago White Stockings. The team is later known as the Colts and Orphans.

1903

The team takes on the Cubs name.

1906

The Cubs win a record 116 games but fall short in the World Series.

1907

The Cubs beat the Detroit Tigers to win their first World Series.

1908

The Cubs become the first team to win back-to-back World Series when they beat the Tigers.

1914

Wrigley Field opens. The Cubs begin playing there in 1916.

1945

The Cubs refuse to let William Sianis and his billy goat into Wrigley Field for a World Series game. Sianis "curses" the team.

1984

Just one win away from the World Series, the Cubs lose three games in a row to the San Diego Padres and are eliminated from the playoffs.

1998

The Cubs' Sammy Sosa hits a team-record 66 home runs, but St. Louis Cardinals slugger Mark McGwire hits 70.

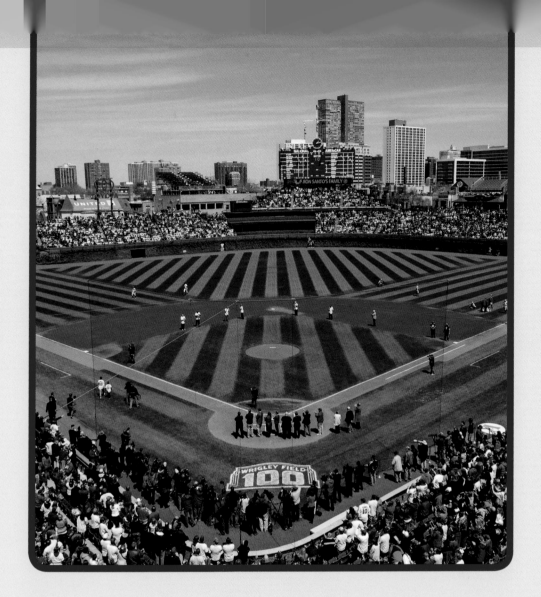

2003

Again one win away from the World Series, the Cubs lose twice in a row to the Florida Marlins and are eliminated from the playoffs after a fan interferes with a foul ball.

2008

A team-record 3.3 million fans attend games at Wrigley Field.

2015

Joe Maddon takes over as Cubs manager. He leads a new generation of Cubs in seeking to end "The Curse of the Billy Goat."

GLOSSARY

ambassador
A representative of something.

attendance
The number of people who go to an event.

ballot
A way of voting.

contend
To be competing for a championship.

curse
A spell or wish for harm or bad luck upon someone or something.

merged
Combined two bodies into one.

pennant
A league championship.

reputation
Public beliefs about someone or something.

retire
To end one's playing career. Teams can also retire a jersey number, meaning no future player can wear that number.

rookie
A first-year player.

trademark
Something that a person is well known for.

FOR MORE INFORMATION

Books

Greenfield, Jimmy. *100 Things Cubs Fans Should Know & Do before They Die.* Chicago: Triumph Books, 2012.

Johnson, Steve. *Chicago Cubs Yesterday & Today.* Minneapolis, MN: Voyageur Press, 2008.

Krantz, Les. *Wrigley Field: The Centennial: 100 Years at the Friendly Confines.* Chicago: Triumph Books, 2013.

Websites

Baseball-Reference
www.baseball-reference.com

Bleed Cubbie Blue
www.bleedcubbieblue.com

Chicago Cubs
www.cubs.com

MLB.com
www.mlb.com

INDEX

Alou, Moises, 5

Banks, Ernie, 6–7, 18, 19
Boston Red Sox, 22, 26
Brickhouse, Jack, 19
Brown, Mordecai "Three Finger," 21
Bryant, Kris, 27

Caray, Harry, 8–9
Castro, Starlin, 26
Chance, Frank, 21
Chicago Bears, 12
Chicago White Sox, 9, 10, 20, 26
Cincinnati Reds, 12
"Curse of the Billy Goat," 4–5, 21, 27

Detroit Tigers, 21

Evers, Johnny, 21

Florida Marlins, 5

"Go Cubs Go," 22

Hill, Glenallen, 25
Houston Astros, 14

Jenkins, Ferguson, 19

Maddon, Joe, 26
Maddux, Greg, 19

New York Yankees, 12

Rizzo, Anthony, 26

San Diego Padres, 16
Sandberg, Ryne, 19
Santo, Ron, 18, 19

Seattle Mariners, 20
Sianis, William "Billy Goat," 4
Sosa, Sammy, 10–11, 14
St. Louis Cardinals, 9, 10

Tampa Bay Rays, 26
Tinker, Joe, 21

WGN, 17
Williams, Billy, 18, 19
Wood, Kerry, 14
World Series, 4, 5, 12, 16, 20, 21, 26
Wrigley Field, 4, 9, 12–13, 16, 19, 22, 24–25
Wrigleyville, 24–25

About the Author

Todd Kortemeier is a writer with a background in journalism and literature. He is a graduate of the University of Minnesota and lives in Minneapolis.

READ MORE FROM 12-STORY LIBRARY

Every 12-Story Library book is available in many formats, including Amazon Kindle and Apple iBooks. For more information, visit your device's store or 12StoryLibrary.com.